A FIRST PICTURE BOOK of NURSERY RHYMES

Illustrated by

ELIZABETH HARBOUR

VIKING

VIKING

Published by the Penguin Group
Penguin Books Ltd, 27 Wrights Lane, London W8 5TZ, England
Penguin Books USA Inc., 375 Hudson Street, New York, New York 10014, USA
Penguin Books Australia Ltd, Ringwood, Victoria, Australia
Penguin Books Canada Ltd, 10 Alcorn Avenue, Toronto, Ontario, Canada M4V 3B2
Penguin Books (NZ) Ltd, 182–190 Wairau Road, Auckland 10, New Zealand

Penguin Books Ltd, Registered Offices: Harmondsworth, Middlesex, England

First published 1995
1 3 5 7 9 10 8 6 4 2

Filmset in New Baskerville

A CIP catalogue record for this book is available from the British Library

ISBN 0–670–85030–6

PRINTED IN BELGIUM BY
proost
INTERNATIONAL BOOK PRODUCTION

CONTENTS

For my dear mother and my three nieces,
Fern, Marina and Natalie

Humpty Dumpty sat on the wall,
Humpty Dumpty had a great fall.
All the King's horses and all the King's men
Couldn't put Humpty together again.

Doctor Foster went to Gloucester
In a shower of rain;
He stepped in a puddle,
Right up to his middle,
And never went there again.

Barber, barber, shave a pig,
How many hairs to make a wig?
Four and twenty, that's enough.
Give the barber a pinch of snuff.

Hickory, dickory, dock,
The mouse ran up the clock.
The clock struck one,
The mouse ran down,
Hickory, dickory, dock.

Diddly, diddly, dumpty,
The cat ran up the plum tree,
Give her a plum and down she'll come,
Diddly, diddly, dumpty.

Two little dicky birds
Sitting on a wall;
One named Peter,
The other named Paul.
Fly away, Peter!
Fly away, Paul!
Come back, Peter!
Come back, Paul!

Hoddley, poddley, puddle and fogs,
Cats are to marry the poodle dogs;
Cats in blue jackets and dogs in red hats,
What will become of the mice and the rats?

Rub-a-dub-dub,
Three men in a tub,
And who do you think they be?
The butcher, the baker,
The candlestick-maker;
Turn 'em out, knaves all three!

Hickety, pickety, my black hen,
She lays eggs for gentlemen;
Gentlemen come every day,
To see what my black hen doth lay.
Some days five and some days ten,
She lays eggs for gentlemen.

9

Sing a song of sixpence,
A pocket full of rye;
Four-and-twenty blackbirds
Baked in a pie.
When the pie was opened
The birds began to sing;
Wasn't that a dainty dish
To set before the King?

The King was in his counting house
Counting out his money;
The Queen was in the parlour
Eating bread and honey;
The maid was in the garden
Hanging out the clothes,
When down flew a blackbird
And pecked off her nose.

Dickery, dickery, dare,
The pig flew up in the air.
The man in brown soon brought him down,
Dickery, dickery, dare.

The little pig went to market,

This little pig stayed at home,

This little pig had roast beef,

And this little pig had none,

And this little pig went, Wee, wee, wee!
All the way home.

Jack Sprat could eat no fat,
His wife could eat no lean,
And so between them both, you see,
They licked the platter clean.

Pussy-cat, pussy-cat, where have you been?
I've been up to London to visit the Queen.
Pussy-cat, pussy-cat, what did you there?
I frightened a little mouse under her chair.

15

Sing, sing,
What shall I sing?
The cat's run away
With the pudding string!
Do, do,
What shall I do?
The cat's run away
With the pudding too!

Pat-a-cake, pat-a-cake, baker's man,
Bake me a cake as fast as you can;
Pat it and prick it, and mark it with B,
Put it in the oven for Baby and me.

Apple-pie, apple-pie,
Peter likes apple-pie;
So do I, so do I.

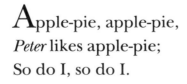

Polly put the kettle on,
Polly put the kettle on,
Polly put the kettle on,
We'll all have tea.

Sukey take it off again,
Sukey take it off again,
Sukey take it off again,
They've all gone away.

Three blind mice, see how they run!
They all ran after the farmer's wife,
Who cut off their tails with a carving knife,
Did you ever see such a thing in your life,
As three blind mice?

Pease-porridge hot,
Pease-porridge cold,
Pease-porridge in the pot,
Nine days old.
Some like it hot,
Some like it cold,
Some like it in the pot,
Nine days old.

Six little mice sat down to spin,
Pussy passed by, and she peeped in.
What are you doing, my little men?

We're weaving shirts for gentlemen.
Can I come in, and cut off your threads?
No, no, Mistress Pussy, you'll cut off our heads.

The Queen of Hearts
She made some tarts,
All on a summer's day;
The Knave of Hearts
He stole those tarts,
And took them clean away.

The King of Hearts
Called for the tarts,
And beat the knave full sore;
The Knave of Hearts
Brought back the tarts,
And vowed he'd steal no more.

Cock-a-doodle-doo!
My dame has lost her shoe,
My master's lost his fiddling stick,
And knows not what to do.

Cock-a-doodle-doo!
What is my dame to do?
Till master finds his fiddling stick
She'll dance without her shoe.

Mary, Mary, quite contrary,
How does your garden grow?
With silver bells and cockle shells
And pretty maids all in a row.

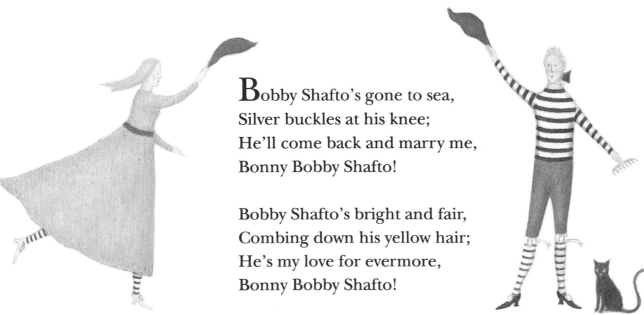

Bobby Shafto's gone to sea,
Silver buckles at his knee;
He'll come back and marry me,
Bonny Bobby Shafto!

Bobby Shafto's bright and fair,
Combing down his yellow hair;
He's my love for evermore,
Bonny Bobby Shafto!

Ding-dong bell, pussy's in the well.
Who put her in? Little Johnny Green.
Who pulled her out? Little Tommy Stout.
What a naughty boy was that,
To try to drown poor pussy-cat,
Who never did any harm,
But killed the mice in his father's barn.

There was a little girl, and she had a little curl
Right in the middle of her forehead;
When she was good she was very, very good,
But when she was bad she was horrid.

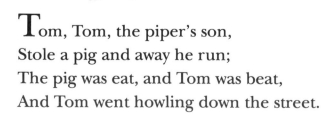

Tom, Tom, the piper's son,
Stole a pig and away he run;
The pig was eat, and Tom was beat,
And Tom went howling down the street.

Little Betty Blue
Lost her holiday shoe,
What can little Betty do?
Give her another
To match the other,
And then she may walk out in two.

Georgie Porgie, pudding and pie,
Kissed the girls and made them cry;
When the boys came out to play,
Georgie Porgie ran away.

Little Polly Flinders
Sat among the cinders,
Warming her pretty little toes;
Her mother came and caught her,
And whipped her little daughter
For spoiling her nice new clothes.

I saw a ship a-sailing,
A-sailing on the sea,
And oh, but it was laden
With pretty things for thee!

There were comfits in the cabin,
And apples in the hold;
The sails were made of silk,
And the masts were all of gold.

The four-and-twenty sailors
That stood between the decks
Were four-and-twenty white mice
With chains about their necks.

The captain was a duck
With a packet on his back,
And when the ship began to move
The captain said, Quack! Quack!

Five little pussy-cats sitting in a row,
Blue ribbons round each neck, fastened in a bow.
Hey, pussies! Ho, pussies! Are your faces clean?
Don't you know you're sitting there so as to be seen?

Higglety, pigglety, pop!
The dog has eaten the mop;
The pig's in a hurry,
The cat's in a flurry,
Higglety, pigglety, pop!

Hey diddle diddle,
The cat and the fiddle,
The cow jumped over the moon;
The little dog laughed
To see such sport,
And the dish ran away with the spoon.

Goosey, goosey gander,
Whither shall I wander?
Upstairs and downstairs
And in my lady's chamber.

There I met an old man
Who would not say his prayers,
I took him by the left leg
And threw him down the stairs.

Wee Willie Winkie runs through the town,
Upstairs and downstairs in his nightgown,
Rapping at the window, crying through the lock,
Are the children in their beds?
For now it's eight o'clock.

Twinkle, twinkle, little star,
How I wonder what you are!
Up above the world so high,
Like a diamond in the sky.